First published in Great Britain in 1990
by Methuen Children's Books, Michelin House
a Division of the Octopus Publishing Group
81 Fulham Road, London SW3 6RB
Text and illustrations copyright © 1990 by
Kady MacDonald Denton
Printed in Great Britain by
MacLehose & Partners Ltd
ISBN 0 416 13012 7

THE CHRISTMAS BOOT

KADY MACDONALD DENTON

Methuen Children's Books

One cold day in December, a few days after
Christmas, Alison found a black, shiny boot.
"Look," she called to Jeremy, "come and see.
There's a boot in the tree."

"I'll try it on," said Jeremy. He tried it first on
one foot, then on the other.
"This isn't right," he said. "The boot's too tight.
There's something stuck in the toe."
"Oh, look!" they cried. "It's a little red ball."

"Here's a spinning top!" said Alison.

"And here's a tiny horse," shouted Jeremy.
"It must be a magic boot!"

"We'll keep the boot," said Jeremy.

"I'll keep the boot. Give it to me," said Alison.

Jeremy and Alison both grabbed the boot
and as they pulled, more presents fell out.
"Look!" shouted Alison.

"Presents!" Alison and Jeremy called
to the other children in the park.
"Look! Presents for everyone!"

"Whose boot is it?" asked the children.
"I don't know," said Jeremy. "Someone has lost
their boot and their presents."

"It's a man's boot," said Alison. "Who do we know
with big winter boots and lots of presents?"

"Father Christmas!" shouted all the children.
"Then," said Alison, "we must give it back."
"But how can we give it back?" asked the children.

"What comes down, must go up," said Alison.
"We need a chimney. Come on, let's go to my house."

Alison told her Mum that they wanted to leave
Father Christmas's boot by the chimney.

Mum turned out the light.
In the dark, all the children pretended to be asleep.
When the children opened their eyes...

the boot was gone!

They all rushed outside to see if they
could find Father Christmas.
"He's already gone," said Jeremy.
"Goodbye, Father Christmas!" said Alison.
"Thank you," called their friends.
"Goodbye. Goodbye."